MW00916071

Will You Play With Me?

The Adventures of Princess Nadia

By Tony Samuel

Copyright © 2011 Antonio A. Samuel

All rights reserved. Published by Talented Books. No part of this book may be reproduced, stored in a retrieval system or transmitted, in any form or by any means without the written consent of the copyright owner. Thank you so much for your kind support.

ISBN-13:
978-0983818212

ISBN-10:
0983818215

First Printing

Published by Talented Books. Leland, NC 28451.
Contact: rescue1one@aol.com. Visit us at www.TalentedBooks.com.

Thank you to Tania and Iz for your valuable insights.
Thank you Nadia for the inspiration to make this happen.

Acknowledgments

This book is dedicated To Nadia.

Daddy loves you forever.

www.TalentedBooks.com

4

Cast

Princess Nadia

Lenny The Lion

Ellen Elephant

Tiny Tiger

One-Eyed Charlie

Snick The Snake

Lazy Allie Alligator

Freddy Finch - The Pretty Bird

About The Author

Tony Samuel is a father and husband. He believes in the rights of children to live happy and carefree lives, while always being encouraged to read and empowered through continuous learning. Tony has a Bachelors degree in Business Marketing and a Masters degree in Leadership. Tony was inspired to write this story for his beloved Princess Nadia.

Will You Play With Me?

By Tony Samuel

$\mathcal{T}$here was once a little Princess named Nadia who dreamed of going on an African safari.

Princess Nadia was ready for her adventure in a wonderful and strange country. She had no fear of wild animals.

One day, her dream came true. Nadia traveled along the wild, grassy and bountiful trees. On her journey Nadia was searching for a friend, so she asked each animal kindly if they would play.

"*W*ill you play with me?"
asked Nadia, smiling the
biggest smile that could be.

"Oh my! Oh me!" snickered Lenny the Lion. "Don't you know I eat people alive? You should run when I arrive."

"Do you want to play right here?" asked Nadia, smiling from ear to ear.

"No my dear," said Ellen Elephant. "Play with someone your own size. You'd steer clear of my path, if you were wise."

" Will you play with me awhile?" asked Nadia, grinning a medium smile.

"RAAAR!" roared Tiny Tiger. "Take a look at my giant paws, and you will see my giant claws."

"May we play here in this place?" asked Nadia with a plain grin on her face.

"*H*a! No way!" laughed

one-eyed Charlie.

"Open my jaws and you will see, rows of very sharp biting teeth!"

"Will you play any game at all?" asked Nadia, with a smile so small.

"Hiss, Hiss," Snick the Snake called. "When I play I like to bite, and when I hug I squeeze too tight."

"Will you play if I jump in?" asked Nadia, barely sporting a grin.

"Chances are thin," snapped Lazy Allie the alligator. "Look at my long and frightening snout! If I were you, I would watch out!"

"No one wants to play with me! Sad and lonely I'll always be," cried Nadia. The corners of her mouth dropped way down, until the princess wore a frown!

Soon a pretty bird swooped by and cried a beautiful bird-like cry.

$\mathcal{N}$adia flashed a little grin and then sadness settled right back in.

"If I can make you smile again, will you promise to be my friend?" asked Freddy Finch.

Freddy Finch squawked and flapped, and landed right on Nadia's lap! Nadia's frown turned upside-down and her laughter echoed all around!

*T*he story spread throughout the herd: a little princess made friends with a bird!

11120341R0

Made in the USA
Lexington, KY
10 September 2011